Kilohana Art League

Six Prize Hawaiian Stories of the Kilohana Art League

Kilohana Art League

Six Prize Hawaiian Stories of the Kilohana Art League

ISBN/EAN: 9783743313217

Manufactured in Europe, USA, Canada, Australia, Japa

Cover: Foto ©Andreas Hilbeck / pixelio.de

Manufactured and distributed by brebook publishing software
(www.brebook.com)

Kilohana Art League

Six Prize Hawaiian Stories of the Kilohana Art League

SIX PRIZE

Hawaiian Stories

OF THE

KILOHANA ART LEAGUE

Honolulu:
Hawaiian Gazette Company
1899

CONTENTS

Kalani

CHAPTER I.

"UHEA oe, Nalima? Elua nahae hou o kuu lole!"[1] "Auwe, pela?"[2] replied the old woman addressed, taking at the same time from Kalani's hands a coat that might best be described as one of many colors. The old man seated himself on the floor of the little hut, and gazed at this same coat in a manner savoring of dejection. "Yes," he said, "while I

---

[1] "Where are you, Nalima? Here are two new rents in my clothes!"

[2] "Oh dear! is that so?"

was digging around the taro down by the stream, I left it hanging on a branch of the big kukui tree, but when I returned to put it on, I found that it had blown off, caught on a piece of bark and torn that hole. Do you think you can mend it so that I can wear it on Sunday? You know I have no other. *Pilikia maoli!*" (sad plight), and Kalani gave a grunt that embodied many emotions.

Nalima's small, slightly withered hands were turning the coat tenderly. Patch had already been placed upon patch, nearly every one differing in material and color from the original fabric, which was a cotton twill, and the bleachings of sun and soap had added variety in many shades of blue and brown.

Yes, she had a little piece of blue flannel left that would just fit this new rent, she mused, and the whole thing must be washed again. She was sure she could have it ready to wear that same night. This hopeful view enabled her old husband to start again with his *o-o* (Hawaiian spade) for the garden patch. He removed his tattered hat as he went, revealing a head of fine proportions. The forehead was high and full, and the top bald and shining. Soft, white locks clustered in his neck, and a white beard several inches in length gave a distinguished look to his face. Patience looked from his soft dark eyes and the expression about his mouth was kind and firm. The small rush mat which Nalima had been braiding when Kalani arrived with his tale of woe was laid aside, and, from a very meager supply of housewifely stores, a needle, thread, and bit of flannel were produced. Her dim eyes strained themselves to adjust the patch to the torn edges, and her trembling hands set the stitches with patient effort. Meanwhile the thoughts of the old wife wandered into the past. The long-ago was a happy time to re-live. When they were young, in Kauikeaouli's time, Kalani had been a *kanaka nui* (great man) among Hawaiians. He had been a *luna* (overseer) in their valley and had directed the *konohiki* (chief's resident land-agent) labor for years. His own *kuli-ana* (land-holding) was a large one, and the rights of the stream for some acres were his. He in his turn controlled the work of others for himself. Their house was large and high and had a window of glass in one end; the *hikie* (bedstead) was a pile of mats soft and fine, and the bedding was of the finest *kapa*.[3] There was always a plenty of *poi*[4] in the calabash; *ti* roots, kukui-nuts, cocoa-nuts and breadfruit abounded for more delicate dishes. They themselves were well and strong, and oh! how proud they were of their boy and girl. Like a dream had been the years between. Sovereign had succeeded sovereign. Epidemics has decimated the people. The *konohiki* labor had lapsed. Strangers had leased the lands, fences now barred the way, and keys effectually locked the fastnesses from the ramblers and seekers for shells and

---

[3] A cloth made from bark.

[4] The Hawaiian "staff of life." A paste made of pounded *taro* root mixed with water.

ferns. Their own acres had been cajoled away from them, and only this little hut far up the valley, and a small plot of land, on which they with difficulty raised a little *taro* and a few sweet potatoes, remained. They were allowed to retain possession of this as compensation for guarding the leased lands of the valley against trespassers, but they received no money. The children had grown and gone. The daughter had married and lived a few years at Kona, Hawaii, then died. The son had braved the Arctic cold and had been a sailor for years on a whale ship. But many, many moons had passed since his last visit home; probably he, too, was dead. They themselves were growing old now; they had no chance to earn money; economy had crystallized for them into the problem of how long they could make things last. Kalani would be broken-hearted when his coat was too old to wear to church, for, rain or sun, he faithfully attended the service at the mouth of the valley every Sunday afternoon, walking several miles to do so. While Nalima sewed and mused, Kalani, wrestling with mountain *nahelchele* (wild growth) was thinking too. Perhaps the vigor in the arm that drove the *o-o* into the grass stirred the thought cells in his head; the mental result, however, was not retrospection, but determination to do some thing in the immediate future to help the present condition of affairs. "I *must* have a new coat. I cannot wear my old one to church any longer. I have no money, but perhaps some one will give me clothes if I ask for them. I have never begged, and Nalima wouldn't let me beg now if she knew about it; I musn't tell her. It is more than two years since I have been beyond the church, but there are *haole* (foreign) families living not far from there, and I'll go to them. I'll tell Nalima I'm going to try to sell some eggs, we've got six saved in the pail, and perhaps I can buy some salmon to bring home to her. It would taste good *(ono loa)* to her. I'll go tomorrow morning." And, full of his resolve, Kalani shouldered his *o-o* and returned to his hut.

CHAPTER II.

"Ruth, please see who is knocking at the side door," said Mrs. Hamilton early one morning in the month of August. "It's a native man, Mamma," said Ruth a moment later, "he wants to see you, but says he can wait until you can come. I think he has never been here before; he is very old; and he has a small tin pail with him." When Mrs. Hamilton opened the door leading to the veranda, the rising sun was glorifying a strip of lawn, glancing among young orange trees, glowing along an hibiscus hedge, and giving an effect beyond description to a golden-shower tree in full bloom. On either side of the steps leading to the drive, banks of ferns stood crisp and cool. The grass was bright with fairy rainbows strung on drops of dew. "Oh, what a morning to be alive!" thought Mrs. Hamilton, "what, I wonder, will be the first thing given me to do this beautiful day?" From the lower step arose, at this instant, Kalani. With the grace and dignity natural to the Hawaiian, he bared his head, and, holding his tattered hat in his hand, gave the friendly salutation "Aloha" which Mrs. Hamilton returned in as friendly a tone. Noting in an instant the splendid proportions of his head, his fine brow, and the character which shone from every feature of his up-turned face, it was with the sincerest interest that she asked in Hawaiian, "What can I do for you, what would you like?" Kalani took a step sideways into the ferns, still looking up into her eyes, and, with various apologetic expressions flitting across his face, finally took hold of the lapel of his coat with his left hand and, drawing it slightly forward, said, "I didn't know but perhaps you had a cast-off coat that you would be willing to give me. This one is very old and has many holes. If I had a better one I should wear it to church and that would be *maikai loa* (very pleasant), but, if not, never mind, it will be all right" *(like pu, he maikai no ia)*. Mrs. Hamilton's quick eye took in at a glance the entire suit in which this son of the soil stood. His garments showed their many patches, and she thought that the colors of the remnants still clinging together, would be difficult to reproduce upon any painter's palette. Stepping within the bedroom door she found Mr. Hamilton adjusting his necktie before the mirror. "George," she said, "do you suppose you have a second-hand coat I might give this man? He needs one badly enough. There is something singularly appealing about him, and, you can see in a moment, he is no beggar."

"Yes, I guess so," said Mr. Hamilton, first taking a glance through the door at Kalani and then proceeding to his wardrobe. Presently he returned and handed his wife an entire suit of grey woolen clothes. "My," said she, "he has asked only for a *coat!* I'll give them to him one by one. Come out and enjoy the good time with me." Returning to the veranda she held up the coat. "Do you suppose this will fit you?" she asked. "Oh yes, yes!" was the quick reply, "you must see for yourself," and his hands trembled as he carefully withdrew the delicate coat he wore from his shoulders. "See, see, it fits, it fits!" (*Ku no, ku no!*) and his hands stroked down the sleeves, and lovingly patted the pocket flaps.

His expressions of delight and appreciation were cut short by Mrs. Hamilton's holding up the trousers. "What do you think about these?" Kalani shot a lightning glance at Mr. Hamilton, who stood on the veranda enjoying the scene, and said "Oh, yes, we are just the same size." "He," pointing to Mr. Hamilton, "isn't any bigger than I am." Taking the trousers, the old man avowed most solemnly that they would be just right *(ku pono loa)*. "Besides," said he with a look of conscious pride, "I've got an old wife who can fix them if they are not." So that point was settled. The vest was now held up. "Of course you don't want this," said Mrs. Hamilton, "it will make you too warm." "A vest, a vest!" he cried, "no it wont, oh, I shall be too proud for anything, (*hookano maoli*) to have a vest!"

All three were laughing by this time, Kalani as much as the others. "Dear me," said Mr. Hamilton, "this is getting interesting. I must see if I can't find him something else." In a moment he was back with a neat, striped negligee shirt, which he himself offered the old man. The expression on the shining face of the native as he received this fresh gift, was something to remember. It was brother looking into brother's face, with a something too deep for words. It was an expression that one would like to meet again, in the world beyond.

"Let's give him a hat," said George Jr., who had joined the group on the veranda, "there are a lot on the hat-tree to spare." The tattered hat under Kalani's arm had not spoken in vain. As the boy was searching for one, his father cried to him, "Bring the silk hat from the top peg." "No, no," said Mrs. Hamilton, "don't let us spoil a good thing by allowing the old man to think we are making fun of him." "Fun of him!" said Mr. Hamilton, "I tell you I know what will please his soul, and it's a silk hat, now see if it's not." George first handed his mother a brown derby, only slightly the worse for wear, and then a silk hat still possessed of a good shine but not the most modern in shape. Having only the first in evidence, Mrs. Hamilton again addressed Kalani. "Do you think you could wear this hat?" "That hat for me? Oh how fine! Yes, yes, I know—" here his words failed, for his eyes had caught sight of the silk hat, which Mr. Hamilton was in a great hurry to prove would be the climax of his life. "Here, try this, I guess you can make it stick on," he said. The brown derby fell among the ferns, and trembling hands seized the shining beaver. *"Auwe, auwe! heaha keia! ka nani! ka maikai! Auwe! ka lokomaikai!"*[5] Over the shining bald head it was pressed, coaxed, urged

---

5 "Oh my! oh my! what's this! how splendid, how fine! Ah, what generosity!"

and settled, and *it was a tight fit.* "There," said Mr. Hamilton, "I told you so, he would wear that hat if it killed him, rather than not take it when he had the chance! Of course he never had a silk hat before in his life."

The old man was speechless and voluble by turns. His good fortune choked him, but the joys of possession ran over his eyes and sparkled in every square inch of his honest face. Ruth brought some wrapping paper, and Mrs. Hamilton helped fold the articles for easy carrying. "But my hat, how am I going to carry my hat?" he wailed. "I'll wear this one," putting the derby on his head, "but this *papale kilika* (silk hat) is to wear to church, and how am I to carry it home?" Another paper was brought, and, with twine, a secure package was made, with a loop to slip over his arm. Then a fresh idea came to the old man. Conscious of the humor of the whole situation, he said, "You have left me only one thing to ask for," and he raised a foot to which was bound a much worn shoe. "Shoes!" cried Ruth, "May I find some, Mamma?" and in less time than it takes to tell it she was back with a pair of half-worn brogans that were more beautiful in Kalani's eyes than the handsomest ten-dollar boots that ever came out of a shoe emporium. Now there really seemed to be nothing left but for the old man to go, but he had something to say.

Lifting his happy face, he said, "You have been very good to me. I have no money to buy such things for myself, and I was going to ask only for a coat. I live in Palolo valley, and have no means of earning anything. I brought a few eggs with me, thinking I could change them for something to take back to my old wife, but now I would like to give them to you." He slipped the cover from his pail and held up to Mrs. Hamilton's view the half dozen small eggs. Tears filled her eyes at his honest, dignified independence. "No, no," said she, slipping a coin in among the eggs, "get something for the wife with the eggs, and give her our *aloha.*"

At last with many an *aloha* and *auwe* of benediction, Kalani betook himself and his new wealth down the drive, and the Hamilton family answered the breakfast bell.

Chapter III.

The barking of a small dog awoke Nalima from a nap. Sitting up, she saw at a little distance down the valley, someone coming up the path. At first she thought it was Kalani, then saw that it was a *haole* hat that appeared and disappeared among the bushes. "*Auwe,* it's some trespasser that's come up here because Kalani is away, what shall I do?" While she yet feared, the figure stood at the door and Kalani's voice reassured her.

We may not repeat all that Nalima listened to, for in another tongue than the Hawaiian, its flavor would be much impaired. The simple souls accepted the great good fortune of the suit of clothes, the shoes, and the hats, with childlike simplicity. The long and early walk had given

Kalani a hearty appetite, which the sour poi, spiced with a bit of salt salmon from the *Pake* (Chinese) store at Moiliili, soon appeased. Nalima produced a few mountain apples she had gathered during his absence, and they felt they had feasted like chiefs of old.

Nor can we tell of the profound sensation produced in the little district church the following Sabbath, when Kalani entered dressed in his new suit, and crowned with his silk hat. This latter he wore until he took his seat, so that all might see it; then he carefully placed it on the bench beside him. It seemed as if the possession of this silk hat bade fair to restore to him his prestige of the long ago. That he should have been in such high favor with anyone, as to receive such a gift, surely argued greatly for his birthright, and for the heritage of his youth, of which the younger generation had not been aware. Certain it was that soon after this Kalani was made a deacon in the church, and other honors were accorded him in the months that followed. In the little hut in the valley, the driest corner was given to the precious hat, and Nalima gently fondled it as she smoothed it again and again, hoping to preserve its shining gloss indefinitely. It was not pride but *satisfaction* in this *special possession* that filled Kalani's soul. He often removed the paper in which it was kept, and, holding it upon his hand, would relate to Nalima the experiences of that momentous morning walk, when he became possessed of this treasure. And Nalima never tired of listening to the tale, though she had long known it by heart. In closing he always said, "The best of it all was, I know they were *glad* to give it to me, and, Nalima, you know what to do with it if I die first."

CHAPTER IV.

"Mamma," cried Ruth Hamilton, reining her horse beside her mother's porch one afternoon a year later, "George and I have been for a ride out to Wailupe and back, and as we came near the Palolo Valley road on our way home, we saw a funeral procession coming down. It passed the corner just as we reached it, and, what do you think! On the *top of the coffin was a silk hat,* and George declares it's the same one Papa gave that old man that came here one morning a good while ago!"

Even so, according to the customs which still obtain in many lands, and which have been handed down through the centuries, of burying one's choicest possessions with the body of the deceased, Kalani and his silk hat were not parted in the grave.

EMMA L. DILLINGHAM.

23

A Legend of Haleakala

W E stood shivering on the brink. At our very feet was the crater of Haleakala, the House of the sun, but that luminary had gone to his other realms and left his dwelling dark, unfathomable and void. No voice of nature was there, no murmuring breeze, no note of bird, no spirit of man or of God moved in those lone and abysmal depths. Only the brilliant stars kept watch above, and they were immeasurable miles away.

We, who stood there in the cool morning air did not add in any way to the majesty of the scene, wrapped as we were in blankets—red, white and gray.

24

"Like lost spirits waiting for waftage to the other shore," remarked the tourist.

"I am sure I have lost my spirits," said a shivering unfortunate, "I think the guide stole them."

"It seems to me we look more like a group of savage Apaches on a bleak mountain summit sketched by Remington," suggested the artist of the crowd.

"Ah, there she blows," cried the first speaker pointing toward the east where a shaft of light had just shot from the dark sea through the gray clouds. We all turned and looked except the newly married couple. They gazed into each others eyes as was their custom.

"I am so cold, dearest," she murmured.

I supposed he furnished her with a share of his red blanket though I was not watching.

"Ladies and gentlemen," said the humorist, "the grand cyclorama of sunrise on Haleakala is about to open, and as a preliminary, I move to throw the poet over the brink as a propitiatory sacrifice to the God of the Sun, who appears to be shocked by our appearance; and besides the poet will attempt to describe this scene and he can't."

"Describe nothing," retorted the poet, "my teeth are chattering so my tongue can't." "Let's throw the guide over, that will propitiate us anyway."

But William, the guide, looked so calm and peaceful as he sat with his back against a rock smoking a short black pipe, that we decided not to disturb him.

Meanwhile the sun rose. He has done this so often that it has become a matter of course with him. But rarely has he risen surrounded with such pomp of circumstance and kingly glory. It might well have been his coronation morning, with clouds of heavy gorgeousness upon his shining shoulders, and the quick heralds of light sent to glorify the distant mountain heights and to awaken the dark and slumbering sea. We seemed to be moving in worlds unrealized as the light swept across the reach of clouds at our feet, broken as a sea of tumbled ice, while around the outer rim rose forms strange or fantastic, the clouds shaping themselves into huge animals or rounding into noble palaces or turning into lofty pinnacles, and on every one the sun had set a crown of flame. The light with glowing hands pulled slowly back the shadows from the crater until it stood clearly revealed in its silence and vastness. From West Maui to Molokai stretched a heavy causeway of cloud beneath which lay the sea dark and glowing like polished porphyry. The sun was above the cloud and the common light of day lay round us.

"Tis past, the visionary splendor fades," remarked the poet, but the remark was not original with him.

Our party now adjourned to the stone house on the summit known as Cruyealcce and after drinking some hot coffee and warming ourselves around the open fire, the humorist and myself testified to our intention of taking William and walking down into the crater. They all said that we were decided idiots, and they would take their exercise out in watching us. The newly married couple said nothing, but looked as I have stated.

"I think that haole can't go down," remarked William, pointing to the humorist. "His legs too thin, they break."

We all laughed except the humorist who could not see the joke.

"Break! you fat rascal," he exclaimed, "before I am done with you, you won't be anything but an animated brown shadow."

With sarcastic comments which did not disturb our serenity and much waving of handkerchiefs we began the descent. We went down at a very rapid gait, the loose dirt smoking at our heels and the canteen thumping against William's fat sides. In a half hour we reached the floor of the crater and stopped to take breath. After William had lighted his pipe we went on our way. First across the black lava flows and broken aa. In the days of its storm and stress this had been the hot and glowing life-blood of the great volcano, but now it was cold, black and congealed. Beyond the flows we came to long stretches of volcanic sands and the lofty cones rose above us, so perfect in form that it seemed the slightest breath of air would disturb their symmetry. Their coloring was wonderful, velvety black, gray and red shading into one another. And through the vast silence the silvery notes of a bird floated down to us from the far battlements of the crater.

After a toilsome tramp we reached the other side where the trees come down the slope, and throwing ourselves down in the shade we looked across the burning plain and enjoyed the coolness by way of contrast as we smoked and took chance shots at stray goats coming down the ridge.

"Do you know any stories or legends connected with Haleakala, William?" I asked.

"Yes, I know one, my grandma always telling."

"That's right, William," said the humorist, "take down your harp from the weeping lauhala trees, and sing to us of the departed glories of your race."

"You see my grandma great old woman, she kahuna, live at Hana. I hear this story every since I was keiki. She says it comes down from some old poets."

And after gazing across the crater for a while William began in his native tongue:

"In former times from the distant Islands of the southern sea came a strange people to Hawaii. On their spears were the great sharks' teeth, and their tabu staffs were crowned with kapa black or white. They were great of statue and became the mois of Hawaii. Then followed a people from beyond the rising sun. Small and broad they were, and came in ships such as were never before seen in Hawaiian seas. But stranger than these peoples was an alien race which came from out the distant north from whence the great trees come floating down upon the rivers of the sea, and the tradewinds take their rise, which come to cool our valleys and the burning sea.

It was in the days when Hua, the impious king reigned in Hana, on the third day before the feast of Lono in the early morning when the fishermen were returning, six canoes came from out a mist that floated on the sea, and moved quickly in even line toward the curving beach. The night before the omens had portended some dire event. The sacrifices had risen from the blood stained lele and stalked beyond the heiau gate, while, from the heights of Haleakala, issued the groanings of the Thunder God. As the aliens strode upon the beach they were taller than our tallest chiefs. Their skins were red as Pele blood that beats within our heart, but their eyes were black as is that blood when it cools upon the mountain sides, yet from them shot fire as the lightning from the thunder clouds. Their heads were encircled by high feather leis which swept backwards almost to the ground. Feathers were they grey and white such as never grew upon the birds that fly within the forests or float upon the sea.

The King took the strangers to his royal hale

and gave them food and drink. There was a woman with them, the wife of their great chief. She appeared like a prophetess, only young. Her skin was pale as the white sea foam. Her dark eyes seemed to gaze afar off, and her smile was like the flash of sun upon the sea. When Hua saw her he desired her for himself and his women became as nothing in his eyes. Therefore Hua urged the redmen to make their home near his hale and they should be aliis in the land though the priest Luahomoe, warned the king that their coming would cast a shadow on his life. But the strangers would not dwell with the king nor with his people, but made their home far up on the slope of Haleakala where the gray clouds ever hang and the white rain falls silently to the ground.

Sometimes when the feather hunters sought the mamo and the oo upon the mountains they would see a figure of one of these men standing on the highest mountain peak against the black clouds as though carved of stone, then, suddenly he would raise his arms towards the sky and a cry would come quick as a javlin piercing to the heart, or, they would hear a rustling in the ferns and see a shape like a red moo moving through the green, but whence it came or whither it went they could never tell.

It chanced that on a certain day their great chief came down to the plain and went to see the king who was stretched at ease in front of his hale on a kapa mat, while the trade winds waved the falling branches of the kou trees like green kahilis above his kingly head. The great chief stood and would not sit upon the matting brought by the attendant. Then the king made a sign to one of his retainers who in a short time, brought several maidens with flowers decking their dark hair, and ornaments of pearl and shells upon their ankles and their arms. They were the fairest in Hua's court. The King waived his hand toward where they stood and said:

"Take these, O chief, they are yours, but let the white queen dwell with me."

Then the great chief folded his arms and looked down at the king while Hua's guard gathered close around him, for there was evil in the great chief's eye, and the king was a very little man before him. Then he grunted 'Umph' and turning left the presence of the king and went quickly to his mountain home.

But Hua's heart was hot within his breast, so he vowed to take the great chief's life and bring the white queen to his royal hale. Forthwith he sent his lunapais into every valley and along the sea to summon the alii and their warriors, but a messenger came the following day from the great chief saying:

"I know your plotting and your heart O King. We will make an end of this matter. Place your kingdom against the possession of the white queen. Choose your mightest warrior, and I will meet him. If I die, take the white queen, but if your warrior dies your people and your lands are mine, O King. But this one condition, I will choose the place where this combat is to be fought."

The crafty Hua thought within his heart, "I will accept this challenge, and if my champion fall my warriors will surround him and his men and slay them. Then the white queen shall not escape me. So he assented. The messenger then took the king and, pointing where the clouds were flowing through the Kaupo gap, he said: "In yonder hollow mountain fights the chief."

The king's heart was troubled then, but he dare not return upon his spoken word. Among the alii there was none so tall and powerful as the young Kuala. In all the sports of peace he was pre-eminent. While in war none would hurl the spear so swiftly, nor use the javlin with such skilled hands, and when he whirled the battle axe above his head none could see it for the speed. He was chosen champion by the King.

For many days the priests consulted the oracles within the enclosure of the sacred anu, but the omens puzzled then, and they said the Gods were not at peace among themselves.

It was on the evening before the day just as the sun sank into the sea, there came a cloud, blacker than the kapa for the dead, moving slowly above the sea, and the gray rain following as a veil behind it. The air around was very still. Then, suddenly the cloud turned to crimson and the mountain and the thousands on the beach were reddened as though by the glow from a great fire. All were frightened, but Kuala only laughed and said, "If it storms now it will be cooler on the morrow." The old priest shook his head and said, "My son, that mountain height will be plenty cool enough for thee."

Late in the afternoon of the destined day the hosts of Maui were gathered in the arms of the great mountain. Foremost stood the King. Around his shoulders fell the yellow mamo cloak, and on his head a helmet yellow as his robe save its crest which was red with the feathers of the scarlet bird. Behind him stood the priests in feather cloaks red as the blood of their sacrifices, while in a half circle rose the hundred alii in cloaks mingled with the royal yellow and the priestly red. As the sunlight shone upon them they were in form and color as the rainbows bent over the valleys green, and on the rounded hills of sand above them stood the warriors thicker than the leaves upon the forest trees, and their thousand spears made the red hills black. A murmur ran amongst them as when the voice of the sea comes on the south wind and the sky is gray. The priests chanted in low tones, the meles of Kuala's race, and waved their arms as they sang of heroic deeds. Kuala stood quietly by the king and looked across the lava plain where, in the distance, could be seen the red men moving, one behind the other, in a line. They came swiftly. When they reached a hundred paces from where stood the king, they stopped and the white queen stood forth before them. Her color was no longer as the pale foam, for the blood beat quickly in her cheeks, and she breathed as though she had been running, while her eyes shone so that even Hua turned his glance away. The great chief stood near her but impassive as though carved of stone. Behind them the warriors stood lean and red with strange colors on their faces, and their heads were crowned with warlike feathers. They moved not, nor looked upon the warriors on the hills, regardless of them as though they were but crawling ants. Then the messenger of the chief advanced across the sand and stood before the king.

"O King, the chief is ready now to offer the victim chosen by you for the sacrifice."

Hua replied, "My champion is here at my right hand, and to-night we will wrap your chief in the funeral kapa, and the black sharks will dine upon his flesh." He would have spoken more but the messenger turned upon his heel and left the king.

Kuala threw aside his feathered cloak and advanced slowly towards the level sand. Then there rose a shout from the hosts upon the hill louder than the thunder of the great waves falling on the beach, and the priests chanted in loud tones beating wildly on their sacred drums. The great chief advanced to meet his foe but stopped, and with arms outstretched towards the sun gazed straight into its burning light while his voice reached to the remotest warrior on the hills, though none could understand the words, so strange they were. Then he turned and faced Kuala, who stood twenty paces distant. All was quiet as is the air before a coming storm. Kuala slowly raised his spear above his head and bending quickly forward sent it with such force that none could see it in the air, but the great chief was quicker than the spear and it went past him deep into the sand. His spear flew so close to Kuala that he felt the wind of its speed upon his cheek. The second time they raised their arms together and send the weapons whirling through the air. The warrior's spear struck some feathers from the great chief's head, whose weapon went straight to Kuala's heart, but before it touched his body Kuala caught it with his hands and turned its course aside, but staggered backwards with the force. Then the warriors cried in lamentation on the hills, but when they saw he was unhurt a shout arose louder than the first. The last spear Kuala poised above his head was of polished koa tipped with ivory, whose point had been dipped in Po's dark waters, carrying death upon its slightest touch. But it never reached the red chief's for the two spears met in the air with a great clash and fell broken on the sand. Then the warriors rushed towards each other and met midway on the sands, their javelins clashing as they met. Suddenly the light had faded while gray clouds covered the crater as with a roof, and the white rain began to fall thick and fast, lying like white stars on cloaks of the alii and of king. Kuala and the great chief could be dimly seen as they whirled around each other in the strife faster than sea birds on the wing. Now rushing together, now stepping quick aside, but Kuala's breathing could be heard by the king and his alii standing near; while the great chief moved quicker than the red lightning from the clouds, without a sound save when his javelin struck the warriors. But moving backward from Kuala's rush his heel struck upon a stone and he swayed slightly. Then the warrior's javelin tore his shoulder till the red blood came. With a cry that made the king and all his followers shiver as with cold, he sprang past Kuala's javelin and fastened his teeth within the flesh and his face was like a demon as he tore the warrior's throat, and Kuala fell slowly back upon the sand, writhing in quick death. Then the Hulumanu, standing by the King, threw his spear and pierced the great chief who fell face downward on the sand. From the hills the warriors came with a mighty rush as slides the land from the steep mountain sides, while the red men awaited their coming with faces lean and fierce. They stood as does a rock within the sea when the great waves surge upon it fall back in beaten foam until one mightier than the rest o'erwhelms it. So stood, so fell the red men on that day.

Hua marked not the raging of the strife but through the tumult pushed his way toward where the white queen stood alone. She fled with exceeding swiftness, moving like a shadow through the falling mist. Hua, in furious anger, raised his spear and sent it straight towards her as she fled. Then the cloud grew thicker and closed around them. Instantly a great cry was heard and the King's people found him bleeding on the sand with his spear point centering in his breast. Whither the white queen went none ever knew. But sometimes the hunter, following his lonely trail through the great mountain, sees a woman's form wrapped in moving mist and with dark hair floating wildly around the pallor of her face."

"That's all," said the guide.

"That's quite a little lie, William," said the humorist.

"I don't know, the old lady says it is just so."

As we started on our homeward trail the clouds had rolled through the two gaps and an opaque mist lay around us. William headed the procession and we had gone about a quarter of a mile and were near the great cone when William stopped suddenly and grasped the humorist by the arm, almost white with terror.

"Look!" he said, pointing towards where the fog had lifted somewhat, and a current of air was whirling the mist, and, in the mist a woman's form and face could be clearly seen. I looked inquiringly at the humorist.

"Can such things be," he said, "and overcome us like a summer cloud, without our special wonders?"

"There are more things in heaven and earth, Horatio," I suggested.

Then we went on in silence through the falling mist, but the humorist took the lead.

GEO. H. DE LA VERGNE.

Peleg Chapman's Sharks

R. DOLE and I were standing in front of one of the caves which are found near the edges of the bay of Hanauma which is situated this side of Koko Head. We were there for several days of recreation. Mr. Dole was glad to get away from the Executive building, where his Ministers had caged various bees in their bonnets. These bees often wrangled with the bees in his own bonnet, and by temporarily separating them, the different bees ameliorated their buzzing, and a general rest prevailed. Mr. Dole said he preferred to take recreation with one who had outgrown the bee-hive age and the age of other annoying human devices.

"Do you see that flat stone?" I asked, pointing to one that lay under some lantana bushes, and was partially concealed by the sand and just beyond the reach of the surf.

"I see it," said Mr. Dole. "Do you think that some person with a bee in his bonnet has been around? Has the stone a story?"

"Well," I said, "that stone belonged to the foundation of a house which Peleg Chapman built away back in the 'thirties.'"

"Tell me the story, said Mr. Dole and he sat down on the grass, as if it were his Cabinet, and stretched his legs out towards the much sounding sea.

I then told him the story as I had obtained it from the most authentic sources, included in which were some scraps in Peleg Chapman's handwriting.

Peleg's father, Silas Chapman, was a poor but honest farmer who lived in Stockbridge, Massachusetts, near the State line. He had been eminently successful in achieving poverty, which he shared generously with his wife and sons. Though mentally dull in most matters, he possessed a rare gift for training animals of all kinds. He was a master of those inarticulate sounds, and musical notes which curiously convey ideas to animals. He talked with his dogs and cats, and made them useful. His trained squirrels brought him abundance of nuts, and his trained robins brought him cherries without injuring them. His cows, pigs, and chickens did curious tricks, and when gathered together in the barnyard, under his voice and eye, were more orderly than the General Assembly of the State. These useful animals did much to relieve the family poverty. The collie dogs stole watermelons and rolled them home, and the tame crows supplied the cattle with ripe corn from the neighbors' fields.

Peleg inherited from his father this singular

gift of training animals, and he had listened to his luminous expositions of the subject.

"Peleg," he said, "all an'mals think. Ef you only larn how they think, you ken do anything with 'em. Each on 'em has a little different way of working his gumption, but you kinder sit along side 'on 'em, get to communin' with 'em in a slow fashion, and you'l find 'em ekal to human critters."

Peleg in due time became more skillful than his father, in training animals. He caught a young eagle over in Lenox, and trained him to relieve the family poverty by stealing chickens over in York State. The eagle was not morally very strong, and often brought home the tough roosters, after eating the tender chickens.

One day, when Peleg was away, the eagle being in a contrary mood, seized Silas Chapman's Sunday coat, and flying away with it dropped it into the Housatonic river. When Peleg reached home, his father told him that the eagle had done a mean job, and that he must pay for the stolen coat.

Peleg refused on the ground that animals had no morals.

"Dad," he said, "you be livin' off them thievin' dogs and birds." Then said his father: "I guess Peleg you and me has got to have some interestin' conversation in the barn, this evenin'."

Peleg acted promptly on this suggestion. At four o'clock, with a small sum of money, he secretly went to the station, and boarded the Boston express. He left a note to his mother saying he was going off and his dad might lick the eagle if he caught him.

On reaching Boston, he wandered about until he reached the Frog pond in the Common. He had often heard that its waters were sacred in the eyes of every Bostonian. Feeling much depressed he took out of his pocket a copy of the Wesminster Catechism, which every child studied in those days, and by accident glanced over the rough wood cuts of Biblical incidents. His eye fell on that of a very stiff looking whale, with a very stiff looking Jonah in front of it, waiting with a very resigned look to be swallowed.

While he was getting some comfort out of Jonah's resigned look, a sea-faring man took a seat by his side, on the public bench, and after glancing at the picture in Peleg's hand, remarked: "purty stiff lookin' whale I guess."

"Ever see'd one?" asked Peleg.

"Caught plenty on 'em," said the sailor. "Been around the Horn and up in the Artic for sperm and right whales. Plenty of lay money too. Down in Wyhee plenty of gals and bananas."

"Goin' again?" asked Peleg.

"Yes, next week," said the sailor.

"Take me?" asked Peleg.

"Guess you can ship on the Julian," said the sailor. "Fresh fo'cas'le hand gets one hundred and fortieth lay. That's his share of all the oil and bone the vessel takes in her cruise. Have good luck, plenty of money," said the sailor.

Peleg glanced at the stiff figure of the whale, closed the book, and said, "I'm goin'."

On reaching New Bedford, he shipped on the Julian, signed ship's articles, and went on board with a new kit. The vessel sailed for the Pacific and the Arctic ocean.

For a few days, Peleg would have been willing to return home and take the vicarious punishment for the eagle's sins rather than sleep in a fo'cas'le bunk. But the ship bowled along towards the equator, and the carefully expurgated yarns of the crew kindled his enthusiasm.

He caught and trained some sea gulls to fetch fish for the cabin and for'rad deck so that his shipmates, instead of calling him a blankety land lubber, took pains to teach him the art of handling ropes, and chewing old plug tobacco, and reading the sulphurous marine literature of the age.

The Julian took five hundred barrels of sperm oil off the island of Juan Fernandez, and finally dropped her anchor in the harbor of Honolulu, for the purpose of getting wood and water and fresh provisions.

On going ashore, Peleg was amazed at the

abundance of bananas of which he was very fond, but for which the price at home was one shilling each. As he gorged himself, he began to think of exchanging his marine interest in the Pacific for a residence on the Islands. He felt justified in deserting, because the air of the forecastle was bad, and the captain had refused to reconstruct the vessel and place saloon cabins at the disposal of the crew. He obtained from Mellish & Co., ship chandlers, an advance of $300 on his lay, and deserted. He concealed himself at Waimanalo, until the vessel sailed for the Arctic, and then keeping out of the way of the native police or "kikos," he crossed over into Manoa valley and followed the coast line from Waikiki towards Koko Head. Finding the secluded bay of Hanauma he remained there. It was surrounded by a high ridge, as it was part of an extinct crater, and one side of it had fallen in towards the ocean, so that it was almost land locked, and the surf and heavy seas rushed through the narrow opening.

With the aid of a native, he laid a foundation of flat stones and built upon them a thatched house. The native brought him fruit and vegetables, and he caught an abundance of fish.

While the Julian was off the island of Juan Fernandez, Peleg had studied the numerous sharks found there. He discovered that the many rows of teeth in the mouth of the female shark were flexible, and rested on elastic gums. They could be laid flat, at the will of the shark. The reason for this curious arrangement was this. Whenever the young sharks are in danger, the mother shark opens her mouth, lays down her teeth, and the young sharks pass over without danger, into a pouch in her body where they remain until the danger is over. He had counted as many as seventy, each of them about three feet long, at one time diving into their mother's mouth, and emerging after the danger was over. He remembered that Prof. Aggasiz or some noted naturalist, had suggested that in some remote period a female kangaroo had tumbled overboard from some prehistoric canoe, and, according to Mr. Darwin, had adapted itself to the new environment, and become a shark. The pouch for the young which appears on the outside in the case of the kangaroo, appears as a pouch on the inside of the shark.

Peleg learned from the natives that at times fish were very scare in the Honolulu market. During the visits of the whaling fleets which often numbered over a hundred vessels, the demand could not be supplied with any regularity. When there was bad weather, the canoes could not put out to sea, and there was a fish famine excepting so far as it could be supplied from the local fish ponds that were entirely owned by the chiefs and King.

Besides there were some rare fish which the chiefs were especially fond of which were found only in deep water and could only be obtained under the most favorable circumstances of tide and weather. Such were the Kawele-a, the Ahi, the Ono and the Omaka. The Ahi was a very delicate fish and was found only off the coast of

Hawaii, and was seldom seen in Honolulu markets.

Peleg said to himself: "Why not train sharks to catch fish? It may be as dad said, some bother to find out their way of thinkin' and they live in the water. But they has eyes and ears, and they hasn't got them things for nothing."

He caught, with the aid of some natives, an immense female shark, and before the young ones could hide, he captured them all, and put them in a pond he built up in the water. He began to educate them. At first they were quite vicious, and refused to be cheerful. But Peleg knew that from the crab to the seraphim, the appeal to the appetite was most effective. After repeated experiments, he found that sharks had a most extraordinary fondness for salt pork. There was a monotony of freshness in their ordinary diet, excepting as a sailor with a rich tobacco flavor, fell in their way once in a while. He also discovered that the addition of beans to the pork made the food especially attractive, and the young sharks quickly submitted to discipline with this reward before them. .

He saw that they thought in their crude way, just as dogs and birds thought, and their hearing was like that of other animals. By tapping stones under water he could call them, but he generally used a speaking tube which he thrust into the water. By using rags of different colors, he trained them to distinguish between colors. He taught them to fetch and carry sticks, and then pieces of meat. As they grew older, he trained them to search for fish in the bay, and to bring them in without injuring them as they took them in or cast them out of their pouches. Pork and beans were liberally used as rewards. He was finally successful in teaching them to distinguish between the grades of fish and as it were, take orders for special kinds and leave the rest. The most intelligent learned to travel long distances, even to Maui and Hawaii, and find the feeding grounds of the rare fish of which he kept samples in a pond, and exhibited to them whenever he desired a supply of that variety.

He never permitted the natives to watch him while in his training school. He gave names to the expert and reliable sharks. His reading was limited so that he selected names from the Bible and from the names of the towns near his home. He called them "Lenox belle," "Barrington belle," "Pittsfield belle," "Lee belle," "Bashbish belle," "Stockbridge belle," and many other Berkshire names were used. The Scriptural names were "Queen of Sheba," "Jezabel," "Mehita-bel" and "Assyrian girl," with other such names. The word "belle" appealed to his poetic instinct.

He graduated the sharks after two years of training, and then opened business. He purchased a canoe, and paddled out to sea, followed by more than twenty submissive fish. He sent them off singly or by battalion, as he called it. In the battalion form, they moved out on an extended line and drove the fish desired towards the caves and small inlets, where they were easily caught, taken into the pouches, and brought to Peleg's canoe, and pork and beans were liberally served out in return.

On the arrival of the next whaling fleet, Peleg entered Honolulu harbor every morning with a large load of mullet in his canoe or with other excellent fish. After disposing of them to the whalers, he put out of the harbor at once, and joined his "sea hounds" as he called them, who waited for him outside the reef. His enormous catches attracted the attention of the natives, who once followed him in the hope of finding his rich fishing grounds. They were especially surprised at his large catch during stormy weather, when they could not go out in their canoes. Nor, by watching Hanauma bay could they get any information, as there were no nets there, and the sharks attracted no attention.

On one occasion as he was paddling along the Waikiki shore after selling his load of fish, he met a fleet of native canoes that had no luck. Taking compassion on them, he dipped his tube under water, gave the sign for mullet to his sea dogs, shipped his paddle, and lit his pipe. In an hour the noses of his hunters rubbed against the side of the canoe, and leaning over, he pulled out of their mouths more than six hundred pounds of mullet, and threw them into the canoes of the natives. The natives were stricken with terror at the sight, and dropped their paddles with the exclamation: "He is a kahuna (sorcerer) of the shark god."

He was soon regarded as an akua (god). No natives dared to enter the bay of Hanauma.

At the end of each whaling season he accumulated considerable sums in gold, a part of which he hid and a part he invested in the purchase of shares in whalers. After the season, he engaged in fishing for the rare fish only, which he supplied to the King and chiefs. Whenever the King said: "Peleg, my friend, I want some of the Ahi," Peleg sent four of his leading sharks to the Kona coast, and they returned within ten hours, with an abundance.

The King sent for him one day and said to him: "You are the most valuable man in my kingdom, and as my predecessors rewarded Isaac Davis and John Young with matrimonial alliances, I would be glad to have you look around and if you see any attractive female of the royal connection that you would like to marry, you may take her until otherwise ordered. I wish for useful men about my throne. I put on no airs, excepting a white cotton shirt. If you accept my offer you are authorized to wear an Admiral's cocked hat, and new boots on State occasion." Peleg replied that he recognized the honor, but that his heart belonged to his sharks and to the daughter of a carpenter who lived near the York State line, and he expected to visit her very soon.

A fanatical native attempted to "anaana" him or pray him to death. He gathered grass and burned it. The oily kukui nuts were thrown on the fire, and the whole resources of the Polynesian Black Art were brought into use. But Peleg lived.

A missionary, hearing of his remarkable powers, visited him and inquired about his ancestors, and among other questions asked him if he had become a heathen and allowed himself to become a kahuna or sorcerer. He replied that he did not hanker after heathenism, but, he said, that if he was in the missionary business he would open a conjuring saloon and beat all their old kahunas at sleight of hand tricks, and that would soon bring the whole crowd over to his side. The heathen, he said, couldn't do much thinking but if they saw him pull a rabbit out of his nose, or take a taro out of a man's ear, they would smash the business of their own conjuring priests. Seein' was believin'. Conjuring tricks would finally bust up their superstitions. The missionary said he and his associates could not look upon the matter in that way, but he would write to the American Board about it, and ask it to send out a respectable conjurer of high moral principle who would hitch a moral to the tail end of every trick, and then challenge a native sorcerer to do any better.

Peleg said that although he was a perverted Puritan, he would supply all of the Honolulu missionaries with fish without charge.

As he had received a very limited education owing to his father's flourishing poverty, he seldom wrote any letters. He did not forget his mother, however. She received from time to time, through Bunker & Co., of New Bedford, comfortable sums of money, with the statement that they came from her son, who was somewhere on the equator, and would come home after awhile. He also sent to Patsy McGloural, who had grown up and did the chores in the family of a rich paper manufacturer, a sandal wood box, and a dress of the finest Chinese silk, which he got from one of the vessels in the sandal wood trade. This dress was the finest in Berkshire county, and when Patsy put it on and went to church, it attracted the attention of the women, so that the preacher gave

out the hymn about being "naked, poor and sin-
ful."

Peleg had invested his money in shares in the
whaleships, which made very profitable voyages,
from Honolulu to the Arctic and Japan seas, and
he became rich for a Berkshire man. After ten
years of fishing he resolved to go home. He
found a young man who came from the neighboring town of Hinsdale, on one of the new whalers,
and after giving him a long trial, instructed him
in the business. He consulted an attorney in Honolulu, and executed an instrument establishing
the "Peleg Chapman Shark Trust," the income
of which was to be used in feeding his faithful
sharks with pork and beans, and in supplying the
poor natives of Honolulu with fish.

He then sailed for New Bedford, and on
arriving there, went directly home. He arrested
the even course of his father's poverty, but did
not inform his indigent but acute parent of the
sources of his fortune. He built for his mother
the finest chicken house in the county, and pres-

ented her with a neat buggy and a gentle horse. He soon married Patsy, and was known as Squire Chapman. As a leading authority on travel, he had no equal in those parts. Subsequently, with the aid of a young student from Williams College, he published in rather Sophomorical language, a book which had a wide circulation titled, "Chapman's researches in the islands of the Pacific."

'Twas Cupid's Part

A Hawaiian Love Story.

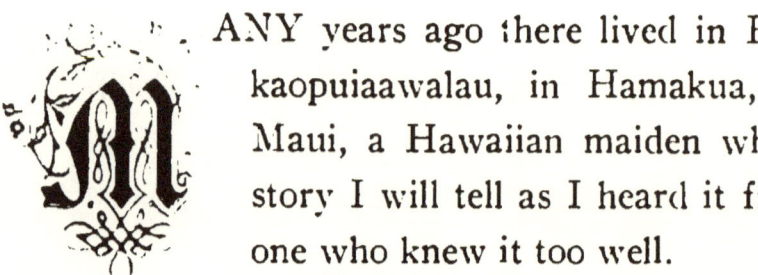

ANY years ago there lived in Hoi-kaopuiaawalau, in Hamakua, on Maui, a Hawaiian maiden whose story I will tell as I heard it from one who knew it too well.

"Her name, which they said was given her by her *kupuna*, Hikiau, who was a favorite chief under Kamehameha the great, was Kalaninuiahilapalapa, but we always called her Lani.

At the time we first met her she was about eleven years of age, very pretty, with regular features and long, black, silky hair. Like many of the natives she had beautiful gazelle-eyes, such as one never tires of gazing into. Probably those eyes cost her most of her—well we will tell it.

She lived with her parents in that beautiful little fern-clad valley, known today as Awalau, where her father worked in a sawmill. He was a very large and powerful man and as good natured as large men usually are.

His name was Kapohakunuipalahalaha, but as that was unnecessarily long, we shortened it to Nui, and a faithful man Nui was at any kind of work. Those who know what sawmill work is know that great strength is appreciated, especially when you are depending on a man to keep his end of a cant-hook up to time. He was as hospitable as the natives have the reputation of being, and that is saying a good deal.

Lani's mother, Kamaka, was a sprightly woman of about thirty-five and did her part to make "life in the woods" pleasant. Neither mother nor daughter appeared to have many household cares and seemed to take delight in wandering up and down the valley in quest of land shrimps, which they caught in a cornucopia-shaped basket made of wicker work. These, with the little black fish named oopu which they found adhering to the stones in the brook, and a fern frond called pohole, together with poi, the Hawaiian staff of life, constituted the principal part of their diet. They were also very fond of pig and chicken and never begrudged the labor or time spent in getting up a luau. From them we had an insight into the Hawaiian mode of living and were surprised to note to what an extent the natives are dependent on the sea for a livelihood. Sometimes Nui would take a day off, whether the master liked or not, and take his family to the beach, when they employed themselves in fishing. They would return with the greatest assortment of shell-fish and fish of many sizes of the most varied colors. Also they would bring limu of several kinds and odors. Limu, you know, is seaweed, and there appear to be as many varieties of it as there are of ferns on the land. There is also a variety of it found in the streams adhering to the rocks on the bottom, which we were always taught to beware of at home, but which the natives eat with cooked meats with great gusto.

They always kept a store of kukui nuts, which they roasted; then breaking up the kernels fine and mixed with salt, they ate it as a relish.

The women took delight in adorning themselves with leis, made either of the maile, which grew in profusion on the steep sides of the ravines, or of the *palapalai,* a luxuriant fern which clothes the valleys as with a garment. Sometimes they would make leis of the fruit of the hala tree, the *pandanus,* which was also very plentiful in that part of the island. Sometimes they would inter-twine the bright hala fruit and the fragrant glossy leaves of the maile, which made a very beautiful lei, especially on an olive skin as a background.

Often we were called in to eat with them and learned to like almost all their native dishes. It was always the custom to call in any stranger passing, to share their food with them. Their style of cooking, viz: under ground, or in a saucepan over an open fire, seemed to give the food a piquancy which had charms for us.

Lani had a very sweet voice and accompanied her singing with a guitar, which she played very sweetly and many an evening we passed about the campfire very comfortably. She could yodel like an inhabitant of the Swiss Alps and often we would hear her singing and yodeling as she came up the valley to cross up to the tableland where we were cutting the large koa trees, preparatory to hauling them to the mill to turn into the handsome lumber so much sought after for making fine furniture. There was not a man in the camp who was not charmed with her.

There was a little Chinaman who came up through our valley, leading pack horses, whose business was buying *pepeiao,* an ear-shaped fungus which is found very plentiful on the trunks of decayed trees on the windward sides of all the islands. The natives gathered and dried these and were always glad to see the Chinaman come around, as they were enabled to exchange them for either cash or the sweet cakes which he carried in his panniers. This fungus contains a good deal of gelatinous matter and was formerly largely exported to China, where it is used for soup making. This poor little waif of a Celestial, named Leong Sing, fell in love with our Lani at first sight and the frequent occasions he took for wandering up our valley were not warranted by the inextensive trade which he found. He made the acquaintance of a Chinaman who had a camp in a neighboring valley, where he was making charcoal from the branches of the koa trees, which he purchased from us. He got to staying over night with his friend and would sometimes join our campfire of an evening and listen to Lani's singing. None of us suspected him of the effrontery of falling in love with our Lani or of expecting her to reciprocate his affection. While at work one day in the woods her father told us that the Chinaman had proposed and wanted to carry her off to Lahaina, where his uncle had a large store. This was a greater temptation to Lani than we suspected, as she was very fond of good clothes and the Chinese are noted for taking the best of care of their wives in that respect. Also was not Lahaina the capital, where young people were numerous and where her accomplishments would be appreciated?

Her father had higher aspirations for his daughter and wished that she might marry a haole.

There was a young man in camp, named Frank Willoughby, (evidently a purser's name) who had come round the Horn in a whaler and had decamped as soon as the vessel touched at Honolulu, as many of our best and worst men did. Frank had a good education and was a very fine looking, healthy young fellow of a most amiable disposition. When Frank heard of the Chinaman's proposal he said he would kill the saffron-colored Celestial on sight and break every bone in his body for his presumption. Then we knew that Frank was badly smitten.

But he was not the only one who was struck bad, as there was a young half Hawaiian-Portuguese named Joe Edwards who was also very denunciatory of the Chinaman and expressed a wish for his speedy demise. Some of us had noticed that Frank was jealous of Joe, as the latter could play the ukeke or Hawaiian Jew's harp, very well, and as a stranger cannot tell what the player is singing on the instrument to his *dulcinea,* Frank could not understand how far Joe had got along in his courtship.

There was another party who was heels over head in love with Lani and this was so utterly unexpected that when the *denouement* took place "you might knock us all down with a feather." This was a big hulk of a black Portuguese named Shenandoah, from his having been captured on a whaler by that Confederate pirate when on her marauding excursion amongst the whalers in the Arctic, from whence he was returned to Honolulu with many others. He was a most repulsive, villainous-looking scoundrel, with black warts on his face; an Iago who could never capture our Desdemona and consequently never came into our calculations.

Anyway the Chinaman's name was "mud" from that time on.

Frank could not talk much native and Lani's English education had been sadly neglected, but it would not be the first instance where love was made with the eyes and not the tongue.

The work in the woods, felling those mammoth koas and hauling them with cattle to the mill, was looked on more as play than work, but we were very tired at night just the same. The *ieie,* an almost impenetrable climbing vine, seemed to take delight in wrapping its rootlets around those koas, to the vexation of the woodsman, and it would sometimes take hours to get at the trunk of a tree. In chopping this ieie the axe would sometimes fly back to the peril of the chopper. Once Frank had the bad or good luck to get cut in the head with his axe and as he bled very freely we were much alarmed and took him down to the camp. Kamaka put a bandage of some native herbs about his head and he remained at home for two or three days. How far his courtship progressed during his convalescence we were never able to learn. Joe said he wished he himself could get his foot cut off or something that he might be invalided.

Sometime after this the boss told us we could all go down to Wailuku for a holiday and spend the Fourth of July, which was going to be grandly celebrated that year on account of some favorable news from home, provided we would take a load of koa lumber down. Horses were not very plentiful with us and we were to ride on the load. As Nui and Shenandoah were to drive the six yoke of oxen and Lani and her mother were to ride we jumped at the opportunity.

The cattle were brought in from the woods, after a tedious search for them, for a bullock can hide himself easier under the parisitic vines and convolvulous which hang from those mammoth koas than anywhere under the sun. The wagon being loaded and the load bound on with chains we eight took our places for an eighteen-mile ride. Lani had provided leis for each of us and she and her mother had collected an immensity of ferns and ki leaves for a cushion to make the soft side of the boards softer, and we had a large hamper of lunch and a merrier party never started for an ox-cart ride.

We got away about 5 a. m., Nui and Shenandoah walking on either side of the team and there never was more fun in a basket of monkeys than on that wagon. He had our old standbys, Nigger and Puakea on the tongue and the young cattle ahead and the trouble these cattle caused "I couldn't be telling." They would dash ahead and fetch up, then they would turn on their tracks and get tangled in the chains, then after a lot of bad language they would get straightened out and make another break, and this was repeated *ad nauseam.*

When we got them up out of the valley and the

74

weight of the load was relieved they made a break to run and almost pulled the heads off the tongue cattle, who, I believe, would sooner have lost those extremities than have been so undignified as to go faster than a walk. Down we went through Kawaiki, and through Huluhulu-nui, Puaahookui, and Kaluanui gulches, the young cattle on the tear and the old ones on their haunches, notwithstanding the chain lock which we had on the wheels. The only thing to hold on to was the binding chain and after getting our hands nipped a few times we preferred to maintain our positions by leaning up against each other. We could not refrain from remarking on the solicitude which both Frank and Joe exhibited for Lani's welfare, doing everything they could devise for her comfort. We have helped tip over a pair of bobs in the snow at home to hear the girls squeal, but we never had an experience of riding on a bullock cart with a trio of lovesick people when every instant produced a bump which would drive a sane person into insanity.

The sun came up right glorious and gave us the benefit of its full actinic rays for the whole day. However, had we been in a palace car we could not have had more fun.

All across that sunburnt plain from East Maui plantation to the beach at Kahului we bumped over rocks and into gullies, for who ever knew of a bullock team fool enough to miss any of those opportunities of getting even on man for his inhumanity to them. Towards 1 p. m. we reached Kahului, the cattle with their tongues hanging out this three hours for lack of water. Here was plenty of it and the whole team rushed into the sea only to find that this fluid which so much resembled water was not the kind they were accustomed to.

Now we were in real danger of getting drowned or getting the wheels stuck in the quick-sand. Frank suggested that we take the wheels off our chariot, the way Pharaoh did and float ashore. He was told to kulikuli and suggest some way out of the difficulty which was feasible. All of us knew how to direct the drivers however, and if they had listened to us we would have been there yet. Nui dashed into the water to seaward of the cattle and striking one of the young leaders on the nose it bellowed with pain and turned shorewards and we were saved, probably for a worse fate. We arrived safely at Wailuku and hastened to relieve ourselves of the superfluous real estate gathered on the way, for the winds of Kahului isthmus can carry more red dirt per cubic inch than any simoon in Arabia, and deposit it more evenly on any obstructing surface.

That evening we met Lani and her mother at the village store and postoffice and she soon became the recipient of much in the line of bright colored dress goods. Frank received a remittance from home and nothing would do but he must give her a side saddle, one of those fancy looking horse-killers such as they sold for twenty dollars. Joe bought her a fancy bridle and another member of the party gave her a flaming scarlet felt saddle cloth. All these to a poor girl who did not own a horse. Horses were pretty cheap in those days, from $5 up. Frank bought her a cream colored mare from a bystander for $20 and placing the saddle and accoutrements on he requested her to mount and try the saddle.

Shenandoah had been buying dress goods at the instigation of Lani's mother and when he came out and saw the beautiful girl mounted on the prancing horse he swore she should never ride it home and commanded her to dismount.

This revelation was too much for us. What; this clod of earth dare to talk in this manner to our Lani? And using tones of authority too! This was the last straw. Frank opened up on him with a volubility and a vocabulary which could only have been acquired before the mast on an American whaler.

Shenandoah dropped his armful of bundles and made a rush at him to annihilate him. Frank had played football too much in college to be badly terrified and when the Portuguese struck at him he lowered his head and rushed his black opponent, taking him just in the short ribs with his head, and Shenandoah was *hors de combat* instanter. It was sometime before he could take a breath, then had to be taken off to a room, which he did not leave until we were ready to return to Hoikaopuiaawalau.

Frank got a nice horse for himself and he and Lani enjoyed the Fourth of July.

At that time there was a fashion among the native women of making their own hats from rooster skins. A fine bird would be selected, no matter what the price ($5 has been paid for a bird for that purpose). The skin was taken off whole and while green put over a mold to dry. Then they would line them and when rightly made one could almost imagine it was a live rooster sitting on a nest. Frank got one of the best of these and gave it to Lani and the next day as he and she rode on either side of the team, for they drove us home, the sight of her was exceedingly galling to Shenandoah who had to ride on the empty wagon, the cock appearing to crow over him at every bounce of her horse.

However the fun was not out of us yet nor out of the bullock. They never seemed to tire giving us our money's worth. When we had arrived at Wailuku we turned them into a corral where there was plenty of food and drink and they ought to have been satisfied. Not so however, for, about midnight a man came to our lodgings and said our cattle had got loose into the cane fields, and, tired as we were we all had to get out and hunt them through the cane, and corral them once more.

We sailed across the plains easily enough but when we came to the region of gulches and night and the rain had set in the anxiety of those on the wagon for their safety was pathetic. We had some marvellous escapes but finally arrived in camp in a half drowned condition.

A couple of days afterwards the charcoal burner came over and told us that Leong Sing had been there during our absence, and says he "there he comes again." That evening he called on Lani and she flatly told him in some expressive way that she wished no more of his attentions. He retired to the Chinese camp and we saw him no more.

The following day the Chinaman came over and asked where Leong Sing was. We said we did not know. Then said he "he is dead for his hat is lying beside the charcoal kiln and it looks as if he had fallen in and been consumed." We went over to see and things did have that appearance, as the roof had fallen in and the pit was a mass of flame. The Chinaman must have taken the rejection of his suit very much to heart to have destroyed himself by such a horrid route.

That same day Shenandoah rode off to Makawao on Lani's horse and reported the death of Leong Sing and swore out a complaint charging Frank Willoughby with the murder.

A constable came over and took Frank away and when the coroner's inquest was held the jury returned a verdict "died by the hands of some one unknown to us." At the examination before the magistrate Shenandoah and Joe Edwards both swore to having repeatedly heard Frank Willoughby threaten to kill the Chinaman and the magistrate held Frank without bail to be tried by the next Circuit Court at Lahaina. He was taken off over the mountains by a policeman. Joe Edwards skipped out for fear he might be also arrested, for his threats were as pronounced as Frank's.

When Frank and the guard got into Lahaina he sent for an old friend of his father's who was practicing law there and he persuaded the Circuit Judge to accept bail as there had been no body found and no cause for the calling of a coroner's jury and that the magistrate merely acted on the hearsay of a pair who were jealous of the prisoner.

Frank went home with Farwell and the latter advised him to return home to New York saying that he had frequently written to him advising such a course and his parents were exceedingly anxious about him. Frank refused to skip his bail and determined to stand trial like a man.

Within two weeks the Chinaman, Leong Sing, came in with his uncle who had gone to search into the matter and Frank was ordered discharged. The Chinaman had felt so heartbroken that he had wandered away up the ravine and climbed up on a ridge and kept on walking until he met a heavy shower and as it is pretty cold up there he turned to go back. Unfortunately he did not take the same ridge down, a thing likely enough to occur, as he had walked so far as to have passed the heads of several ravines, and keeping too much to the right had brought up the following night at Halehaku, some six miles from his point of departure. The natives took care of him and in a few days he was enabled to get a horse and return to camp to the agreeable surprise of the rest of us.

Frank took Mr. Farwell's advice and went straight home to New York. Years afterwards we were riding from Waihee to Lahaina by way of Kahakuloa and arriving at the latter village we felt as if some fish and poi would taste good. It was a dilapidated looking place and the shanties were hardly improvements on pigsties, but we decided that it was better to eat there than to risk going farther and finding none.

We stopped at the best looking shanty and were told they would prepare us some *opihi*, a shell fish abundant on the rocks there, the sale of which is about the only source of livelihood of the few inhabitants.

Imagine our surprise when we were called to eat to find that our hostess was none other than Lani and that Shenandoah was our host and that their eleven little black offsprings were the kids we saw perched on the fence.

Lani was an old fagged out woman without any traces of the belle she had been, and Shenandoah was blacker and uglier than ever. "Apples of Sodom," said my friend, and we paid for our opihi and po. and departed.

J. W. Girvin.

Hiku i Kanahele

BOVE the long sloping hills of Kona where the coffee grows luxuriantly, on the stately mountain of Hualalai, he lived, this Hiku I Kanahele. That he existed there can be no doubt, for the Kamaainas will tell you the most remarkable stories concerning him, which have been cherished with all the old-time love of romance to the present matter-of-fact age, handed down from generation to generation. They will tell you also that his father Ku was a Demi-God and his mother Hina a Demi-Goddess, and will eagerly show you a ro-

mantic relic of the past at the foot of the mountain, the Ke Ana o Hina—Cave of Hina, and will point out to you on the Kona coast, not far from Kailua, with its soft, dreamy warm atmosphere and enchanting bay, the palace where Hiku and his bride resided.

Ku and Hina had two children: Hiku, kane, and Kawelu, wahine, she being many years his junior. Hiku, however, did not know of her existence, for when a very little kaikamahine she was given to the care of the brave Chief of Holualoa, who reared her as his own child.

Beautiful as the sunrise was Kawelu, with eyes as large, soft and brown as the heart of a sunflower, tall, and graceful as the palms which swayed in the murmuring breezes in her palace garden, with a disposition sweet as the maile wreaths and ohia leis her maidens wove to adorn her jet-black hair, or wind around her willowy shapely form.

Many were the young chiefs who sought her favors, but for all she had only smiles of friendship, though at times, with the wanton coquetry innate in the heart of every beautiful woman, she would smile archly and invitingly upon some handsome Alii, then regard him with a saucy indifference which made her doubly precious in his eyes. Agile as she was beautiful, her equal could not be found throughout the Isle in athletic games. Often, in the pastime of throwing the spear, had she evaded half a dozen of these dangerous weapons cast at her at once, catching some with her hands, warding off or eluding the others. None could hurl the arrows so dextrously as she, nor ride so swiftly on the holua down the steep hills, and few cared to leap from such lofty rocks into the swollen streams; and she would think it a light task to swim for miles upon the gently swelling waters of the blue ocean, saying with a merry laugh that the dreaded Mano was her good friend. But the pastime she loved best of all was surf riding, and so wondrously expert was she in this exhilarating sport, and so beautiful did she appear standing erect on her board on the crest of an incoming wave, breaking in snowy foam all around her, so like a radiant Nymph or Goddess freshly risen from the seething waters, that the onlookers would burst into thunderous applause, calling her Kawelu the Beautiful, which was borne echoing up the mountain for many miles; and it was there in his home on the mountain top that Hiku heard these strange sounds wafted thither by the vagrant winds. Often had he asked his mother what they meant, but always evasive were her answers, for well she knew, with her wonderful power of divining the future, what the result would be if he should know. But at last, so persistent were his queries, she told him the sounds he heard were the voices of the people, applauding the most lovely wahine in all the world, praising her beauty and skill as she rode on the waves, and that this beautiful maiden was his own sister. Then a great warm desire filled his breast, and he said: "I must go to her; I must see this charming sister of mine, and ride with her on the waves." With commands and entreaties Hina endeavored to detain him, but to no purpose. Then she told him they would fall in love with each other, and that would bring great pilikia, for it was considered then a proper thing for the chiefs to make love to and marry their own sisters.

The next day Hiku departed for the coast with a surf board made by his father. Being descended from the Gods he had all their innate beauty of form and cleverness; and the manner in which he rode the waves called forth the plaudits of the assembled crowd again and again.

Kawelu, who at this time was indolently lying on the royal mats in the palace, her shapely form being lomilomied by her attentive maids, inquired why the people applauded so heartily, and on being told there had come a stranger to the shore as strong and graceful and athletic as a God, and that he was riding her favorite nalu, which were tabu to those not of Royal birth, hastily encircled her slender waist with her pa'u, and with the Leipalaoa around her neck (an ivory insignia of royalty enclosed in human hair), hurried to the beach, and there upon the white gleaming crests of her own nalu saw the most handsome youth her liquid eyes smiled upon with a malo around his loins, borne swiftly towards her, landing almost at her feet. Their eyes met, and both stood still as though transfixed by some delightful sensation, then with a sudden joyous impulse she took the Leipalaoa from her bosom and threw it around his neck, expressing a desire for him, it being a privilege, graciously accorded her royal station, to ask whom she pleased to be her lover. Hiku with all the fervor of the poetical nature returned her impromptu affection, for she appeared to him like one of his beautiful ancestors, who were Gods and Goddesses, of whom Ku and Hina had told him marvellous stories in his boyhood.

The happy lovers repaired to the Chief, the foster father of Kawelu, and when he learned of Hiku's exalted station readily gave consent to their union.

Several months sped swiftly by, never had time tripped along so merrily, his jaunty footsteps being hastened by hilarious luaus where hulas were sung and danced; and throughout the happy period the two lovers nestled together like a pair of cooing doves, never out of each other's presence. None amongst the hundreds of guests could dance the hulas with such ease and grace, nor sing so harmoniously; and when linked arm in arm as they rode on their surf boards on the hissing breakers, their handsome forms erect and stately, they seemed to the wondering gazers like the offspring of the Gods from some mystic realm beyond the waste of waters surrounding their tranquil isle or from one of the millions of moving worlds that shone above at night, which ever filled them with awe and amazement.

But there comes a time in the sweetest moments of our lives when the causes which induced them cease to operate, when Love itself grows tired of loving. Hiku had never before been so long away from his parents, and having drank to satiety of the love of his graceful Kawelu, a strong yearning filled his heart to see his mother

Hina, a yearning which increased daily, till at length he told his affectionate bride that he must leave her for awhile. With tears and entreaties she implored him to stay, fearing this was a ruse to abandon her, that he no longer wished her caresses; but he became sullen and obstinate, and one day at sunrise he stealthily left the couch of his sweet young wife, whose eyes were softly closed in blissful slumber.

Kawelu awoke; Hiku was gone, and whither? Perhaps forever? These were the thoughts which swiftly filled her mind, and caused her eyes to weep rivers of tears. Then she wildly prayed to the Gods to bring him back to her aching bosom, and finding no response, set out alone along the mountain trail towards his home, where she surmised he was journeying. But Hiku with his natural intuition knew of her design, and calling to his aid the clouds he bade them intercept her path, and the rain he bade fall to make slippery the ground for her feet, and the branches of the trees and the ferns and vines to detain her. Despite these obstacles, with all Love's fond foolishness, Kawelu followed her recreant lover for many hours, to sink at last exhausted on the cold wet earth, her soft skin torn by the thorny bushes and branches of the ohias, and her long silken hair tossed wildly around her form where the ieie vine had clutched it as she passed. Salt tears flowed from her eyes; her rosy morning dream of Love had vanished, and the black despair of night had taken its place. Calling loudly in the unbroken silence of the forest for her lover, she chanted the following lines pathetically:

Pii ana Hiku i ke kualono,
Ka lala e kau kolo ana;
I keekeehiia e ka ua,
Helelei ka pua ilalo,
E Hiku hoi e,
Hoi mai kaua e!

Which roughly translated are as follows:

Hiku has gone up the mountain,
Where the long winding branches are creeping,

And the blossoms fall thickly around
Where the rain on the branches is weeping:
Oh Hiku! come back to me!

The radiant tropic morning has dawned, the
sun has kissed the raindrops from the faces of the
flowers, but on the sweet gentle face of Kawelu
the raindrops of her heart still fall unceasingly!
Vainly her father tries to soothe her grief, for he
had found her weeping and shivering on the lonely mountain side; vainly her maids cluster around
with soft words of condolence. At length she
sleeps, and they leave her, praying to the Gods to
take away this great sorrow, to make her again
the warm ray of sunshine, gladdening all with
which it came in contact. When they returned
Kawelu was dead! Grieved beyond endurance by
her tragic loss she sought release in Death for
this maddening pain her heart could never hold,
fastening with her own gentlefingers around her
smooth round throat the death-inducing cord!

Hiku had greeted his mother Hina with a kiss,

but she bent upon him reproachful eyes, and said "My son, you have killed your sister; already she lies dead through loss of you! You must now go and try to undo the great wrong you have committed." Then Hiku in despair rushed down the mountain accompanied by Ku, and reaching the palace of his beautiful Kawelu found his mother's words to be true, and with loud manifestations of grief had her body placed in a dark cool room which was tabu to all.

By his superior intuition Ku discerned Kawelu's soul had gone to Aina Milu, a region of pleasure in the underwood, a place where the spirits of those who break Nature's laws go at death, where no sun ever shines. The entrance to this realm of shades he found to be in the fertile valley of Waipio, and thither he and the now distracted Hiku swiftly sped, gathering as they went the Kowali vine, weaving of it a stout rope. On the side of the valley they discovered a large hole (pointed out by the natives to the present day) which Ku said was the entrance to this darksome world of festive spirits. Hiku unwound his huge coil of rope with the delicate blue and white Kowali flowers entwined in its strands, and prepared to descend into the dark pit. Previous to doing so, however, he provided himself with an empty cocoanut shell, and rubbed his body all over with some rotten kukui nut oil, which emitted a most offensive odor, and with a kukui nut for a light, whilst Ku firmly held the rope, he descended into the blackness.

On reaching the bottom he found himself in a gloomy region amidst thorny trees without leaves and fruit, dry and barren, with a close heavy stifling atmosphere, whose odor excited the senses and produced an intense thirst. Countless numbers of spirits were gathered there, all active and restless, engaged in the very games they were fond of on earth. A great luau was being prepared, where thousands of phantom pigs and chickens were cooking in fires that gave no light. The Demon King Milu was going that night to marry a beautiful fresh young soul who had just arrived in his weird realm; and looking towards the throne of the king Hiku in dismay saw she was none other than his own lost bride.

Much excitement was created by the presence of Hiku, but he smelled so badly of the rotten kukui nuts that the spirits did not care to approach very closely, designing him "Ke akua pilau,"—the bad smelling ghost.

The merry game of Kilu was going on at the time, and in a few moments his presence was forgotten in its absorbing delights. The game is one of love, a wahine taking in her hand a small ball, with which she endeavors to strike the kanaka she desires, chanting at the same time a verse of a song, and if successful he becomes her immediate lover.

Kawelu was still seated on the elevated throne, holding in her dainty fingers the little ball which was the promoter of this intense merriment. Her mobile lips were chanting a cooing refrain, one which she and Hiku together had composed on earth in the glad days of their grief wedded life.

In the midst of it she stopped, and he took up the chant, all the others remaining silent, as the song was unknown to them. Instantly she called in a tremulous voice, "Who is this that sings;" as though some forgotten memory had wakened in her soul. No one spoke; then she left her place and went amongst the throng, looking into each face until she came to Hiku, who was crouching low, when she stopped, but finding in him a bad-smelling ghost she returned and recommenced the chant. Again she paused a moment when half through, and once more Hiku took up the refrain. Kawelu was intensely agitated; this time she observed it was the bad-smelling spirit who chanted the remainder of her melody, and again approached him, but he during this time had made a swing of his long rope and was swiftly swinging backwards and forwards, to the delight of the clustering spirits who had never seen anything of the kind before. "How smart the bad-smelling ghost is," they said, whilst Kawelu clapped her hands delightedly at the performance, expressing a desire to get on the swing; but Hiku, disguising his voice, said "this is a very difficult thing to learn; you might injure yourself seriously if you tried it without my help; if you sit in my lap I will swing you, then afterwards you can swing by yourself." But the swinging spirit smelled so strongly she would not accept his invitation until they had placed a long wrapper around him, when she did as he suggested. Higher and higher Hiku sent the swing; with all the strength of his nervy, muscular, frame he propelled it back and forth, holding Kawelu close to his heart the while, which was beating rapidly with trembling hopes. Suddenly he pulled on the rope, the signal agreed on with his father to haul him up, and immediately, still moving in long tremendous sweeps, the swing rose high in the air, higher and higher each instant, amidst the alarmed shouts of the subjects of Milu, whose shrill cries echoed gruesomely along the avenues of foliageless trees, "He is stealing the King's wahine, he is stealing the King's wahine." Milu leaped madly forward to snatch her from his arms, but slipped on the Kilu ball, which lay on the ground, he fell heavily forward, and was trampled under the feet of his excited minions, and swift as were their movements, the marvellous strength of Ku, hauling up the swing, was more availing, for it shot up the black shaft with lightning rapidity, the startled Kawelu struggling wildly to escape, Hiku clasping her tightly to his breast, holding her easily in his strong grasp, chanting some mystic words whereby she became smaller and smaller, until he held her in the hollow of his hand, when he forced her into the empty cocoanut shell, and holding his fingers firmly over the hole safely returned to earth, glad to escape from the gloom of this underworld of unyholesome mirth and ceaseless revelry. Quickly they turned their faces towards Hualalai, looking in the distance like a dark ominous shadow, and before many hours their anxious feet echoed in the chamber where lay the mute body of Kawelu, still under strict tabu, no dog having barked in the vicinity of its sacred precincts, nor foot of man passed by the spot, since their departure.

The spirit leaves the body through the eyes, through the little holes in the corners of the eyes nearest the nose, when Death calls it. This Ku and Hiku knew, but they also knew that the spirit cannot return in the same manner, that it must find its way, if ever it returns, into its earthly tenement of flesh and blood through the hollow in the sole of the foot. Placing the cocoanut there, and removing his finger from the hole, Hiku commanded the spirit of his beloved Kawelu to enter her body, lying there so pathetically cold and still that the tears sprang to his eyes as he gazed. The spirit went as far as the knee, when it returned; again he commanded it to enter, and this time it went to the hip, but could go no further. Once again he commanded the spirit to seek an entrance, and with fluttering heart and motionless limbs awaited the outcome of those terribly anxious moments, for well he knew how many were the chances of the soul being lost in the intricate channels of the body, then to his unbounded joy he perceived a slight pulsing movement of the eyelids, then a gradual unveiling of her liquid dark-brown orbs, as she murmured, "Why did you wake me; I had so pleasant a sleep; why did you not let me rest;" but when she felt the warm-impassioned kisses of her lover on her cold lips, and heard his voice sounding in her ears like rare music she vaguely remembered having heard before under sweet conditions, breathing protestations of affection and love, and when his warm tears of joyous thankfulness fell on her smooth velvetry cheek, she awoke to a full realization of the tranquil bliss of love, of the delicious unspeakable harmony poets vainly endeavor to describe, remembering vividly the weird events of the past few days, and her arms twined lovingly around the form of her own Hiku, on whose trembling bosom she softly nestled.

Centuries have passed; Hiku and Kawelu no longer exist on this plane of action, but whilst the

Hawaiian race endures will live the story of their love, and the spectral past with its warriors and gods, and its warm love and worship and song and story will ever be brilliantly reflected in their hearts. The lovers lived to a mellow old age, ever faithful to each other, blessed with a numerous offspring, from whom the kings of Hawaii claimed descent. And the old kamaainas will earnestly tell you that every bit of this romantic story is absolutely true.

MAURICIO.

Story of a Brave Woman

HREE riders came out of the woods, and, turning into the road leading from Napoopoo to the uplands, slowly began the ascent. As they went up, the long plains, reaching from the forest covered heights of Mauna Loa to the ocean, seemed to grow broader, and the sea rose higher, till the far away horizon almost touched the sinking sun. Lanes of glassy water stretched from the shore into illimitable distance. A ship lying motionless looked as if hanging in mid-air. Under the cliff the delicate lines of cocoanut and palm trees were silhouetted against the ocean mirror. Far to the south ran the black and frowning coast, relieved here and there by white lines of foam creeping lazily in from the ocean, only to look darker as the surf melted from sight. On the plain, little clusters of trees, or a house, or a thin curl of smoke, indicated the presence of men: and back of all rose the forest, vast, dim and mysterious, stretching away for miles till lost in the clouds resting softly on the bosom of the mountain.

Such a scene could not fail to arrest attention, and, though our riders were tired, they reined in their horses to enjoy its quiet beauty.

"What a wonderful scene! I have been through Europe, feasted my eyes on the Alps, and have seen the finest that America can produce, but I never saw its equal," said the tourist.

"It looks as if such a picture might be the theatre of thrilling romance and history" said the Coffee Planter. "Is it not here that Captain Cook was killed? And I think I have heard that a famous battle was fought somewhere near: the last struggle of the past against advancing Christianity."

"Yes," replied the Native, slowly, with a lingering look in his eyes, as he turned from the inspiring view to his companions. "Yes, this is all historic ground. Over there under the setting sun, at Kuamoo, was fought the battle of Kekuaokalani, and there a heroic woman braved and met death with her husband, a rebel chief. On these plains below and on yonder heights there have been many thrilling scenes in Hawaii's history. But all of the romance is not in the past. Do you see those houses away down the coast, this side of the high lands of Honokua? See how they glow in the setting sun-light. That is Hookena, and only a few years ago it witnessed the last act in a simple drama, which can hardly be excelled in all the tales of heroism in the past. It was told me in part by the woman who was or is the heroine, for she yet lives. And I looked at her in wonder, because she was so unconscious of it all."

"Let us hear the story," said the Planter. "We will sit on that high point and watch this glorious scene fade into moonlight, while we rest and listen." They dismounted and stepped from the road to a projecting rock and, throwing themselves on the grass where none of the wonderful vision could be missed, listened. The Native looked a little embarrassed at his sudden transformation from guide to story-teller, but accepted the position and began.

"Many years ago a native family lived a few miles above Hookena, on land which had been occupied by their ancestors for generations, for they belonged to the race of chiefs. The house was hidden from the road, in the midst of a grove of orange, bread-fruit, mango, banana and other trees. It is on storied ground, for many stirring events in the past history of Hawaii had occurred here. A son and three daughters were the children. They received more than the usual care and attention given to Hawaiian children, and had grown to man and womanhood serious and reflective. The young man, Keawe, was filled with a desire to do something noble for his dying race. Though he had travelled over the Islands and had been well received everywhere, yet he was heart-free, and said he would never marry, but wait untrammelled till his time for action should come. With eagerness he watched political developments at the capital. His heart beat wildly when the last Kamehameha died, and Kalakaua was elected King. Such a method of King-making did not suit his chivalric ideas. The records of personal prowess, of brave chiefs and noble women were his delight. He mourned that such records belonged to the well nigh forgotten past. His ambition was not ignoble. He wanted the Hawaiians to be worthy of the best civilization, to maintain a Hawaiian kingdom, because that the native was equal to it. While he mourned, he condemned the frequent failures, under which the native was forfeiting the confidence of his white friends. He was one of the overwhelming majority who regarded Kalakaua's accession as unworthy, and as the beginning of the end of Hawaiian supremacy.

One day, while fishing at the beach where he was doing more dreaming than fishing; sometimes idly watching a laughing company of girls who were bathing and surf-riding; he was startled by a cry of terror. Springing to his feet, he saw that one of the girls was desperately struggling to swim ashore, where her affrighted companions were running wildly about crying for help. Looking toward the sea he saw a large fin on the surface rapidly following the swimmer. Accustomed to every athletic sport; perfectly at home in the water; always cool and self possessed, he saw, that to overtake her, the shark must pass a low rocky headland, and in an instant he was there with a long knife in his hand. He remembered seeing the face of the girl as she struggled desperately to escape. There was a single terrified glance, but he saw a beautiful woman, with a face indicating a higher type than usual. There was no time for admiration. The shark was turning and, with a horrid open mouth, was about to rush upon its victim. He gave a loud shout, jumped full upon the huge beast, and in an instant had plunged his knife to the hilt again and again into its body. Then he was hurled into the seething brine, as the frightened animal with frantic plunges rushed seaward. Coming to the surface and looking about he saw the body of the girl near by. He thought her dead. She was indeed stunned and hurt, for the shark gave her a fearful blow in turning. It was the work of only a minute to drag her out. There for a moment he saw the full measure of her youth and beauty, but did not wait for returning consciousness. Seeing that she was recovering he walked swiftly away.

But he was wounded, and, denounce and reproach himself as he would, the sweet face ever and anon came before his eyes, and sent the blood tingling and dancing through his veins. He tried to crush out the image, and determined to enter into active life; to cease dreaming, and begin then and at once to accomplish his high aims.

The political campaign, culminating in the election of 1886, had commenced. Kalakaua had announced the aim of his reign: to increase and develope the Hawaiian people. "Hawaii for the Hawaiians" made an inspiring war cry. Keawe entered with energy and hope into the conflict. Yet it troubled him, and it seemed as if there was something wrong in opposing the noble Pilipo, who had so long faithfully represented the people of Kona in the National Legislature. But Kalakaua declared that Pilipo must be replaced by another man, and was himself coming to assist in the conflict. With the ancient faith and confidence in the chief, Keawe put aside his doubts and worked day and night for the success of the holy cause. It was holy to him and as the day of election drew near, his belief grew stronger, that at last a deliverer had come and Hawaii was to be redeemed. Already he saw, in a bright future, a government by Hawaiians with full friendship for all nations, and cordial relations with those who had helped his people into the best light of civilization. The King came, and with him a troop of palace guards from Honolulu. When all of these were, by the royal will, duly registered as voters, and means, other than argument and persuasion, were used to help on the good cause, a chilly sense of something wrong cooled Keawe's ardor. He met the King and was cordially received. His heart bounded with pleasure at words of praise for his work. An invitation to a feast and dance was accepted, and only when he went and saw, did he realize the mockery and sham behind the fine words. Heart sick, dizzy with a sore disappointment, early the next morning, when all were sleeping, he mounted his horse and stole away, alone. The cold mountain air relieved the pain in his head, but his heart was weary and the future looked dark. He saw that if there was momentary triumph, all the sooner disaster must come; and he longed to know how to avert the danger. He grew weary thinking and trying to hope, and his thoughts went to other things. Again he was in the water, struggling to save her life. Again the sweet face appeared before him, so fair and gentle. The sun was hot now; he had ridden for hours, and, alighting, threw himself on the grass and looked up through the leafy bower at the bright sky. Perhaps he slept; at any rate he dreamed that a sweet voice was singing "Aloha oe." He sat up and listened. It was not a dream, and a strong desire to see the face of the singer possessed him. The voice drew nearer, then she passed near by carrying a pitcher, and went to a spring. It was the girl he had saved from the shark! She wore a loose flowing gown of white, and a maile branch twisted about her head hardly confined the silky hair which floated down her back. A coral pin held the gown at her neck. Short sleeves only partly hid her graceful and shapely arms.

Keawe arose and stood watching. His heart beat tumultuously. No other woman had so strongly moved him, and now he would speak and not run again. A movement startled her, and rising with the dripping pitcher in her hand, she turned and saw him. That she knew him was instantly evident; but her eyes modestly dropped and she moved as if to go. But he was in the path, and, seeing that, she hesitated and turned to go through the woods, but could not and stood again, looking at her feet which just peeped from below the gown. Keawe stepped towards her and said, "Do you remember the shark?" "Yes, I know you," she replied. Her eyes said more and he saw it again. As he stepped nearer she said, "Why did you not let me thank you? I thought you might come." It flashed through his mind that he had wasted two months pursuing an ignis fatuus, only to have nothing but bitterness at the end, when it might have been ————! "I was afraid to come," he replied. "I wanted to work for Hawaii and our people." "Yes, I know," she said. "You have spoken bravely. All Kona trusts in your words!" "Did you believe them?" he quickly asked. "Do you believe in *me*?" A look was her reply. "Will you believe in me if I say that I have done with 'Hawaii for the Hawaiians', under such leadership?" "I will always believe in you. But come, you are tired. My father will be glad to meet you" she said quickly. "May I drink?" he said, and held out his hand. She gave him the pitcher, which he held and looked at the pretty figure standing near the spring. "You are Rebecca at the well." "And are you Abraham's servant?" "No, I am Isaac himself," he replied and tried to take her hand. "Oh! but Isaac did not meet Rebecca at the well!" And, laughing merrily, she ran down the path towards her home. He followed but though he wanted, the opportunity for other words did not come; she was so coy.

It was not the only visit. Very often did business calls take him along that lovely mountain road and there was always a welcome at the home of Lilia. He told her of his love, and in April they were married.

They built a little cottage which nestled snugly in a quiet valley on the mountain side, and there they passed a few months of perfect happiness. All loved them. He was regarded as the wise adviser and friend of the country-side. She became the gentle sister of those who were ill, or suffering or wayward, and their home was the center of an influence which helped and lifted.

But a shadow came into their lives. He grew silent, reserved, almost afraid of his beautiful Lilia. She watched with eager anxiety and entreated his confidence, but his lips were sealed. Only his tremulous voice and shaking hand betrayed suffering. Sometimes she fancied that his hands grew palsied and his bright eye was dim, but repelled the fancy with terror. One day he came home with such a look that her heart stood still, and words died upon her lips. He gazed into her eyes with passionate agony and, taking her hands, said "Will you still believe in me if I say we must part; that I must leave you and go away, and you must stay here and live out your life—your precious life, so dear to me—all, all alone?" Then her courage came, and she said, "No, I will never leave you. You are mine. I must go too, wherever you go!" "But," said he, "I have seen the examining surgeon to-day, and he says that I must go by the next trip of the steamer to Honolulu." And then the full measure of her woe dawned upon the stricken wife. With unutterable anguish she threw her arms about his body and clasped him tightly to her breast. "I was allowed to come here and prepare to go, and to bid a last farewell to all I hold so dear. I shall never see these trees, the flowers, this house, my friends, nor you, my precious wife, again." But her face had grown hard and stern, and, relaxing her hold, she told her plan. It was to take him into a far off deep recess in the woods. There was up the mountain side a deep crater, overgrown with trees, ferns, vines and a wild luxuriance of growth, which kindly nature had draped so softly that its hideousness was lost. It was considered inaccessible, and only the family knew of an ancient lava cavern which entered its deepest recess. One of several mouths of the cavern was near the house. "But the law says that I must go" he urged. "There is no law higher than my love for you," and he yielded to her imperious urgency. Quickly and stealthily she carried there such articles as the simplest life might require, and a few days later, when the officers of the law came, Keawe was not to be found and no one knew where they had gone.

With untiring love the wife watched and aided her husband. Together they built a little bower out of view from the upper edges of the crater, under the spreading branches of a kukui tree. A little pool, fed by the constant drip from the over-hanging wall, supplied them with pure water. Near at hand, under a mass of ferns, maile and ieie, was the mouth of the cavern. She grew familiar with its turns and windings, till she almost dared to brave its black recesses without a torch. In one of its dry and sheltered windings, she stored articles of food and clothing, thinking that sometime a watch might be stationed at the home on the hill-side, and she could not venture out. But days melted into weeks; weeks became months: two years passed, and their hiding place was not discovered. No one came, though Keawe often longed to see the faces of friends. But they were afraid to venture near and the cavern echoed only to her feet, and the silence of the deep pit was only broken by their voices and the music of birds. At times, a sudden gust rushed down the steep sides and every tree waved and bowed its head, and the leaves of the banana rustled and quivered. The sunlight only touched the bottom in summer and then for a few minutes only. But it was not gloomy, the glorious sky was always there and the brilliant light, and bloom and fragrance filled the air. No, it was not always bright, sometimes tempests whirled far over their heads; trees in the world above tossed their branches over the abyss, leaves and twigs fell gently, or branches, and once, a tree, were hurled down with deafening noise. The roar of thunder, and vast sheets and torrents of rain filled the pit. Once, in a still night, they were startled and terrified by a sudden boom far below their feet and the earth shook, stones rattled down the rocky sides of the abyss, and they remembered the dread power of the volcano. "It is Pele! she is angry with us!" cried Lilia. "No," replied her husband, "we have thrown ourselves into the protecting bosom of the Goddess! We are safe in her arms." They were safe from human sight and interference, and Lilia's soul feasted in the presence of him she loved. She poured out upon him such a wealth of devotion, that a miser might have envied. But alas, though safe from man, he was under the fell power of disease, and slowly yielded. Day after day he grew weaker and less able to help himself, until the fond wife performed the most menial tasks. But they were not menial to her. Every thing for him was a glory and a joy.

"I cannot last long" he said one day, "and I want you to have my lands. Get your mother's young husband, the lawyer, to come, that it may be settled." He came, and, looking wonderingly about, prepared a deed which he said would accomplish the object. Keawe was not satisfied. "It sounds wrong—why should the name of your wife appear? he asked. "She is your wife's mother," was the reply, "and you cannot convey to your wife direct. When this deed is recorded my wife can then convey to your wife. You must hurry or it will be too late," said the coming man. With some doubt still, but trusting to his friend's good faith, knowing he was alone cut off from all the world, Keawe signed, and the deed was taken away. Patiently they waited for weeks to finish the business, "and then," said Keawe, "you will have a home." But the lawyer did not come, and evaded Lilia's eager questions.

One day when returning to the cavern, her heart stood still as she saw slowly emerging from its mouth, several police officers, bearing on a rough litter the helpless form of her beloved Keawe. At a glance she saw the whole base deception. Her step-father had betrayed their secret hiding place, and the end had come! With a frantic wail of despair, she flung herself at their feet and begged and implored. But her entreaties were vain, and the sick man was taken to Hookena where the steamer was waiting. At the landing. as the boat drew near the shore, she learned that he was to go alone and then her grief knew no bounds. As he was put on board and turned imploring eyes on her, she made a desperate attempt to go too, and in her struggle her clothing was almost torn away. The officers of the law thought they were doing their duty, but their eyes were full of pity. "Keawe! Oh Keawe, my beloved husband!" she cried, "let me go with you!" But no answer came. The steamer turned her head towards the sea, and he was gone. She fell to the earth, and lay with buried face for many minutes. It seemed to her that nothing was left and bitterly she mourned her loss. But suddenly starting, she asked eagerly for a horse, which was furnished at once by a sympathetic friend. Mounting, she went without stopping for rest or food until, on the second day, Kawaihae was reached. Soon a steamer came, and she went to Honolulu, only to hear on landing that Keawe had died on the trip down. Giving way to despair, she dejected sought the house of an aunt, where she was kindly received, and there she remained for several months."

"And that is the story," said the Native.

"It is rather sad, but she was a heroine sure enough," said the Planter.

The pale light of the crescent moon served only to render the landscape shadowy. All nature rested: An owl fluttered slowly by and a soft murmur from far below told that the restless sea alone moved. There was no other sound. The riders mounted and silently stole away.

THE NATIVE.